Juba

Mika,
Thanks so much.
Take Care,

Some of these poems have appeared in the following anthologies, chapbooks, and periodicals: *Catch the Fire* (Riverhead Press), *gawd and alluh huh sistahs*, and *when we were mud*; *African Voices*; *NUVO* Magazine; *Sinister Wisdom*; *Rap Pages*; and *Rag Shock*.

This book may not be reproduced in whole or in part, except in the case of reviews, without permission from

Wildheart Press
P.O. Box 1115
Jamaica Plain, MA 02130.

Cover image: *ansiosa* copyright ©1998 laurie prendergast
Interior design and production: laurie prendergast

The text of this book is set in Adobe Garamond (Adobe).
The cover font is Basketcase (B. Haber).

Printed on acid-free paper in the United States by GoodWay Graphics, Burlington, MA.
First edition.

Library of Congress Cataloging in Publication Data
Neely, Letta, 1971-
  Juba: poetry/by letta neely

Library of Congree Catalog number:
98-90181

ISBN 0-9663097-2-3

Juba

mountains

DIRT

magic

music

dance

fire

poetry by letta neely

Wildheart Press
jamaica plain, massachusetts

Contents

Dedicated to my Brother
Christopher Kenyatta Neely
who makes me laugh
and
who has always liked me
unconditionally

america: welcome to Colonial Parking

1. Trenches

This room
is filled
with children
whose minds
are parked
whose bodies
flirt in
war zones

this--line--do--not--cross--this--line--do--not--cross--this--line--do--not--cross--this--line

they can
memorize
chalk lines
give a
litany
of names
understand
the bulk
of dead;
cannot
define
living

In this
room words
are a
montage
of strange
symbols;

words—the
art of
them on
the page—
are elusive
but phrases
filled with
double
entendres
fall from
their mouths
makes me
know that

sometimes
they sneak
past barriers;
conceal
boxcutters
in their
teeth

Do not
tell me
this is
an accident

that this
is fate

Do not
throw Darwin
at me

come instead
to read their
hungry eyes

Walk to the bodegas
and liquor stores that lock us
in like backward army forts
no one passes the borders
no one—not cats nor progress—
passes the borders without scars

Now then
tell me
where this
begins
and ends
tell why if i
ask keon to
read he gets so
angry
he screams
BITCH BITCH
CUNT
then

arrives
early
the next
day volunteering
to erase
the board

Tell me about lead paint
Tell me about repression
Tell me about powerlines
Tell me about people layered horizontal
Tell me about dumping bodies over ships
  about bones in seas
  and how this is
  genetic anger
  at death
how it has
crept inside
his dreams and
does not leave
him in daylight

Then go further
back and forward
and tell me how bear
was talking to spirits
how on hot days
pine cones scream

REVOLUTION

and their seeds
pop into air

Coda

It never starts with bloodshed/
like it's talked about/
not with the scalpings and slaveships and suicides/never
begins with auschwitz or the naked body of that last womon
found
in central park
doesn't begin with this paper or 3 mile island
the stories do not open up with chernobyl or chemotherapy
or crack
...Always begins with a dream of a
dream   elements
swirling together and loving
the company of motion
loving the feel of energies rubbing
up against and inside each other
it always starts with a dream of travel
of what this rubbing will manifest
it is sexual
this birthing of existence
from dream
afterwards no matter what
there is always
memory

2. *Genesis revisited*

After god took over
serpent was the first revolutionary
serpent was smooth, slithering through memory to give Eve
some answers
tasting memory and talking to the recently dead and about
to be born
to get the message right/nothing sour on her tongue to pass on
to Eve
Eve was not impressionable she was in love
with serpent's description of memory and
she wanted to taste
serpent was harriet and pedro albiso campo
serpent was audre and the blizzard of '96,
serpent was cricket and crow and this baby child
on rikers island
screaming in the waiting room
serpent was knowing the tree in the garden knew all the
waves of memory
serpent was knowing the tree in the garden reached through
time and
could smell color, could taste sunset
serpent knew the tree in the garden made love to the moon
each and every night
serpent knew revolution depended on love
and that the tree in the garden was a real gawd
like we are all real gawds
and that this so-called god was behind a curtain pulling strings
and building walls
around earth and saying: *garden, welcome to my garden*
like the whole earth wasn't green and in love with itself
the serpent knew this god was a greedy fraud wanting attention
a playground bully who cried when i punched him
a government whose existence depends on borders

serpent was a union organizer   a mob buster   a coltrane song
a freedom march
serpent was the grunt of the preacher
was a lover coming out of the closet
whispering sweet everythings to Eve
serpent was an incantation
serpent who knew green on the outside
of god's garden knew a jail
when she saw one
she set on letting her people go
Come here,
she said, sliding her tongue
along Eve's hand
Follow me, I want to show you something sweet

3. borders

guantanamo or bedstuy
the borders surprise desire of freedom   ceiling no longer glass
but virtual reality   *i can actually stick my hand through* you
think   so you plunge like it's a bird it's a plane
it's freedom   and all the alarms go off and this net you
didn't see drapes over you   you are a criminal
you were trespassing   didn't you see the signs
didn't you know not to stray far   from your homeland
didn't you know   freedom   was not your home

so you put a lid on everything   don't explode   diffuse your mind
separate from spirit   let your hands refuse to
acknowledge your fingers   separate everything into piles   box
these piles   make labels   put everything in the back of the
refrigerator   push the refrigerator next to your bed   turn on the
refrigerator   dream within its incessant hum   someday you will
dig a hole in a lot littered by people who do not know their beauty
bury the refrigerator   but for now microwave dinners, frozen tater
tots, and canned greens suffice   match the drab paint   peeling
from your insides

you could have used the creamed corn
to patch your walls but you are comforted
by the sight of blood   something about
the pain reminds   you   you longed
for freedom once   once nearly tasted
sky

for a second you recall:
the cold wind was necessary and hot
enuf to keep you reaching

through the net with your screams
for a moment you remember:
you heard your own voice
for the first and then the last time
within a fragmented second

when the net branded you
poor and destined for lines
again

and sometimes when you
roll over to sniff another line of

coke into your nostril

another line of standing
disappears

and it is all vague
        how you grew up believing
        the smiling moon followed you to your
        grandmother's and withstood
        your father's drunken ramblings
        it's all clear and murky after that

                        after the dreams of
                        touching begin to haunt
                        you and the decision to
                        run or stand is only yours
                        you become
                        you become
                        afraid to reach for sky again;

to touch that laughter
which shatters
murkiness and pain
the laughter that is indistinguishably music
and sobbing
the laughter that leaves letting pain
reconnect through your body like
highway junctions   like blood clots
leaving tight knots like history
in your shoulders and lower back
you learn to numb
the fragmentation
refuse the laughter
hate the temporary

4. *Insistent Memory*

the sky has been trying to break through
buildings to reach you
nobody ever told you this
except the womon
no one would let you touch
        stay away from her   they said

        she drinks too much   *she's a crackhead*
                                 she's insane
you remember this time

you were 12 and walking home from the corner store
with a 35¢ fruit punch faygo pop a 35¢ snickers bar
some dreams you were humming inside your
head   and the milk you were sent to buy for cornbread
you remember:
she walked up next to you
a little drowsy   and tipsy
and said   *what are you singing?*
              you brushed past her thinking
       she is crazy   *i wasn't singing anything*
all the while
you were making
recipes in your head
for escape of his reach   his
manifest destiny on
your island of
a body   this singing you remember
             later that night
             when you need the recipe   and
             cannot recall it

Dream #6

we   were
forced to make fire
our enemy
hands
feet
tied
our flesh burning off bone
was the last smell
we   were always
plotting even in
our silence
did you not see freedom
in our eyes,
I heard fire sing "this is not my choice"
as our skin went up in smoke

       I heard the limb resisting the insistent
       pull of gravity, I heard henry defy death
       his last breath was freedom   then
       the sound of men's fingers rummaging in his mouth
       snatching teeth and tongue for souvenirs, heirlooms
       to document former wealth. I heard henry's ear
       ripped away and tucked into a pocket
       his body hit the ground and they rushed
           to
                cut
      pieces   of rope
                          from
           round
               his neck
          to save
          to reminder
          to document

I watched children at the picnic
awed at the slowness with which reluctant fire
eats skin.   amazed at a rope's power to
suspend and swing a grown man
in mid air; I watched them count the
minutes
the wind holds and cradles
screams

I saw them repulse at their parent's
grinning unfazed by the wind's howling.

I heard adults laughing
telling their children not to turn
                                            their
                                            faces

I remembered before:
the earth was strands of music
and color waving inseparable aloneness   we were drum and
continental shelf, others were drum and volcano,
drum and coral reef, drum and cumulus cloud and chant
we stomped our feet   drum and island,
we waved our arms through wind archipelago, isthmus
drum and river and swamp, rainforest drum
we were all stepdancing fancy
drawing in the dirt with our bare feet

it was the foul stench of greed that
crept between marrow and muscle
amoeba and crest of wave; that makes
us snatch our own tongues from each
other's mouths;
sever our feet from ankles.

tell the children not to turn
away from this
and the
smell
of our burning flesh

hollering for a memory

as
all these churches
goin up
in flames

"There is a kinship among these things.... They're not burning
down Black barbecue joints, they're not burning down Black
pool halls.... They're burning down Black churches. It's like
they're burning a cross in my front yard. They're burning
symbols of resistance and community, hope and refuge."
— Randolph Scott-McLaughlin

somewhere in the bible, it say
                faith without works is dead
somewhere in the bible, it say
                faith without works is dead

and we're askin "who?"
when we should be askin "why?"

                fallin down on our knees
                talkin to the klan, saying "please,
                        don't burn our
                        temple
                        down"

when we should be askin "why?"

why what?
                why this baptismal burning?
why what?
                why this baptismal burning?

and the spirits might say
                    did you witness aids?
and the spirits might ask
                    did you witness hunger?

and we askin "who?"
when we should be askin "why?"
                    why this baptismal burning?

                    and what i want to remember is
                    sleeping inside cardboard boxes
                    did not bring outrage

                    that swollen ankles and blistered dreams
                    that guantanamo
                    did not bring outrage

                    and the spirits might say
                              did you witness
                              pain?

                    i want to remember that
                    nigeria
                    somalia
                    haiti
                    rwanda
                    ethiopia and
                    starvation and hunger and children
                    eating lead paint from peeling walls in
                    east harlem
                    do not bring outrage

that we have not brought outrage
for a long, long time

when we should be askin "why?"

why what?

why this baptismal burning?

i want to remember
that terri jewell did not
that brandon teena and
marsha johnson did not
that mutilated brown gay men did not
and women found bound
in houses, dead in the trunks of cars
did not bring outrage

i want to remember that even
oj simpson mike tyson colin powell
do not bring outrage

witness this, my people

witness this baptismal burning
burning this empty sanctuary of us
I say walk
walk into this cleansing fire

walk into the fire asking
where were you, where were you church

when michael stewart was killed?
why didn't you lay hands on roland's,
on sabah's,
on quinifa's lesions?

where were you church

                when that idena showed up
                with bruises at yo
                front door?

where were you church
when you were needed, when you were needed?

                i want to remember
                that my mama's pain
                did not bring outrage
                that the fact that he couldn't read
                does not bring
                outrage
                that poverty does not
                that multicolored crack vials and
                tracks in her arms
                do not bring outrage

witness

                that the pastor had a beautiful car

witness this baptismal

                and preached powerful sermons of
                complacency

witness this fire

                that the ushers came
                for tithing 5 times and the hungry
                still went home hungry

witness this fire

                walk into,
                lay down on
                burning embers

gawd and alluh huh sistahs

on dat great gittin up mornin'
gawd and alluh huh sistahs
wuz weavin theyselves a fyne tuesday
some fixin breakfast for each other
and some still in bed ringin in da mornin' slowly/softly

one sistah said to another, "it's so much light in heah, we
need some shade"
"ummmmmm hmmmmm," they all went, even the sistahs
who wuz lovin said, "ummmmmm hmmmmm" and got off
           the clouds
    to join the circle that wuz forming

the sistahs all gathered round each other into a circle and
began callin
  colors into the sky
         chantin
            "sunloveshe i found a place to lay my head
earth deep resonant
        blackness empowering soulful blackness a
        happyblacksong pulled
           from blackness
              to blackness beautifulpowerful
                  comfortinglovingblackness"

and one tall sistah started spinning round
        with her dreads flying round her and circles of
    green and blue   purple and blue
        wuz trailing round her with gawd and alluh
huh sistahs shoutin
           and clappin

"it's you my sistah, it's you, you bettah go on girl wit yo bad self,
it's you girl,
        go sistaaah, go, go sistaaaaah go, go sistah go"
    and that tall tall ebony sistah raised her hands through the
sky and stretched her feets in the dirt till they became roots and
        she say
        "sunloveme i found a place to lay my head
earth deep resonant
        blackness empowering soulful blackness a
        happyblacksong pulled
            from blackness
                to blackness beautifulpowerful
                    comfortinglovingblackness"

                and don't ya'll know soon it wuz
            nightfall and alluh a sudden there wuz this
            sound of crickets and
                    waves reachin
                all the way up to them clouds where gawd and
alluh huh sistahs
            wuz braidin and twistin each other's hair
            and makin up songs
for the second day we didn't git to read about in no
            bible neither

when we were mud

under this traffic and concrete i am standing on soil
that Otter molded when Yemaya wet it
once maybe nothing had a name
not Otter or ocean or mud or moon
we took things for what they were
order was just their very existence
not their names
if a name came about
it was used, maybe everyone
had their own sounds for what they saw, felt, dreamed
but i'm sure there were no words like president
or king, owner or lease, or landlord

especially in this city, puddles and sidewalk cracks
sprouting green warriors
make me smile
just to glimpse at sky playing hide and seek
amongst these unwieldy catacombs
keeps me balanced

in nyc, midtown, Seagull is the only being
close enuf to Yemaya to speak of her existence
Seagull flies overhead, circles twice
and keeps going in a direction
i cannot follow now
i go instead into one of the catacombs
and kneel to an altar/sacrificing my soul for
rent money

there once was a time
when Otter and Yemaya
molded and carved
trees and wasps and us
when land was only land
and powerful
when there was no need for sacrifice
of tree or soul
think about this
now
we strip trees
dye them the color of leaves
and put white men's faces on them
to pay for places to sleep
there
once was a space when Otter
and Yemaya molded
us
when
the order of
things
was
not
so painful

Sonnet for the Ogoni People's Struggle

Do not forget their names, the way they left
This earth hanging   onto beliefs shouted
Across the waters. They said, "We exist,
Though they slaughter us and drain our land's blood

We lay our bodies on the land to feel;
The bit drills into blood, then bone, then oil
Bosses have full pockets but unclean—
able hands. The trees, rocks, and sky will roil

Back in disgust, refusing to be chopped,
Broken and choked. But for now, the earth has
Yet to claim greedmongers and those who hop
Back and forth—complaining, but buying gas

She will welcome us as revolution
We will become earthquakes of reminder."

Connections

There are connections between us
between the lines we've needed or been forced to draw with our
blood
across
time space words wounds
On these new york streets i've seen cracks in the sidewalk and
grass spurting through like revolution holding fast
to one creed only: "keep going, keep going baby, keep going."
The crabgrass makes me think about where we,   you and i
are going
it's a hard day when i realize i don't know any of my enemies
personally
It's my friends i'm speaking to
somehow we keep fighting the same battles over and over again
and arguing over
who's got it worse   who's on the bottom of the totem pole
and i don't mean to
proselytize
but we're killing each other
and
the totem pole is still standing
and
we're still using it
not knowing it's an ethnic slur

Me, i feel trapped in the middle of all this whirlpool
i feel like i'm on top of three mountains
shooting
at myself
I went to the march on washington and saw a lot of white men
together

talking about we will no longer sit on the back of the bus and
somebody had the nerve to say:
"there are a million rosa parks' here"
and i thought
it's not about white guilt or even gay pride
but make sure the
truth
is being told
Cuz the rosas couldn't make it to the march and
as for the back of the bus
whoever thought it up probably
flew
first class

So, i'm not talking bout not aligning with the struggles of my
Blk peoples cuz i understand the connections all too well
just remember to take Emmit Till, Atlanta child murders,
Smallpox blankets, Stonewall, the treatment of
Chinese railroaders, and Apple pie
all together

Every day in harlem i face a different kind a fear
other Blk peoples screaming at me with their eyes
cuz i'm in love with way a womon is

One time a man said to my friend, he stood next to her and said,
"I love you
cuz you Blk and you my sistah, but I think all faggots and dykes
should die."
One time a "friend" said to my sister in the presence of enemies,
"You're not natural"
and then wanted to know
why she felt
unsafe

I want to know does anyone fully comprehend this tapestry
does anyone know how to sew all this together without mixing
histories or
trading truth for slogans.
We are not all hanging from trees
                    standing in welfare lines
                    neck deep in sand getting our heads kicked
                    off into the sunset
                    (these things are being done as we speak)
We are not all getting beat down at Stonewall
We are not all being dragged from our homes by our hair
                    being raped by husbands
                         or friends
                         or lovers
We are not all dying the same way.
But we are all fighting to breathe
                    fighting to breathe

The logic of kindergarten

We want to reduce this to lines
to straight edges to signs and stickers and billboards and slogans
            act up fight aids

We want to make quilts that won't keep us warm that are too
big and too real for our frail museums

We want to blame somebody the haitians the homosexuals the
drug addicts the dreamers the sinners We want a reason

We want to wear ribbons
We want to have a minute of silence a day without art

We want to auction diana's dresses
We want to block bridges

We want to chant   silence=death or action=life
We want to have parties on fire island

We want to have celebrities
We want to keep on being america

We want to half-truth safe sex
We want to half-lie love

We want to wrap ourselves in latex
We want to forget that we can't remember all the names
We wanna know who did this? Whose fault is this?

We want to say this is the apocalypse We don't want to look at this
We want more acronyms

We want to rally   We want to run
We want to say it is their fault

29

We want sex skin to skin again
We want to hide

We want to take out our checkbooks and sign on the bottom line
We want joycelyn elders

We want to keep all our privileges
                        We want
                        to be
                        in the
                        front of
                        the line

We want to accessorize aids
We want our souvenir t-shirts that say I survived 1997
We want silver collector spoons and all the books and videos ever made

We want shrines
We want to know t-cell counts and new therapies

We want to trace track lines on her arms
We want to count his lesions

We want to get what we can
We want our contract in fine print

she wants her mommy back
she's five years old with her keys around her neck

standing at the front door standing
reaching tippytoe to turn the knob, reaching tippytoe to turn the knob

Mostly We Merge

Mostly we merge into each other inside rooms
and obvious distinctions blur
      like when your thoughts
      brush across my mind before
      your voice enters my ear
I am in love with these moments
when our different skins become seamless
      like tide meeting sand,
when our visions strengthen sight
I am in love with moments when
      taste brings us to the middle
      of dirt and trees and sky

There when the sun has gone down
and the moon is steady
  we can give birth to me
  and though I have
  already seen cormorant standing on sea rock
  raising glistening black wings to sun
I have never been inside its laughter,
      its mouth meeting water
      until now
we can give birth to me among waves of sound, color, energy, spirit

Yet outside we are often numb—senseless and invisible to each other
This is a hazard of our love
how a sudden stifling can rise up between us like projects   breaking
sky   into   allotted   views   from   barred   windows
      we become strangers
      frightened of this prison thrown up grotesquely
      in the middle of our power
    it's not growing

we can't tend it
it's not ours
        instead it's a cement of knots
        twisting us like the gnarled
        fists of an elder
        widowed by her dreams

We are lost then
We have lost then the intrinsic map
to the terrain of each other's spirit
and mind and body
instead we have become peoples in a new place drumming
unheard across 5:15 nyc traffic

If you would/I would
hum, make a wave, sing a song
reach your hand in mine
on a crowded street corner
over the cement
        We could find our path again
        We could
        We know this still
we are afraid sometimes
to touch
each other
so afraid that our most familiar can become
alien too quickly; without preparation

afraid of drought
afraid that if we touch here
someone will slam us into traffic

Myself, I have visions of being shot for wanting to love you on a
street corner
Afraid that if we touch here—hand to hand over cement—
we will be killed
this is a hazard of our love

                    And yet we manage
                    to find water and sunrise
                    to carve rivers of hot water
                    into cement
                    to sail us back
                    inside each other
                    to where our voices
                    mingle
                    without sound

In this country where my brother is imprisoned

There are no miracles in boundaries.
Everything I have ever loved reeks of freedom—
Yet my fear sometimes keeps a grip as familiar
And as haunting as
Stale air on a greyhound bus

How do you love a country?
You love its landscape: the way Sky dances with
Tree, the way Rain falls down and Sunflowers begin
tiny like the nail on your baby finger and if you let them breathe
they become yellow giants singing praises to Sun

If we neglect all our relations we will not survive
The building up of walls will continue inside of self
We will carry imprints of this structure/the mottos of
stagnant power will leap from our mouths like commercial jingles
If we forget to meet each other's eyes, we won't survive
the intruding numbness
I tell you,
Already I am surrounded by streets and city anger all day long
and at night, sometimes the noises stand on the
sidelines screeching,
　　　　"We know what you really want"
to all the free womyn dancing in my dreams

I stay because of Children
and because where I live there are Red Wing
Blackbirds, Crows, and Sparrows all over who talk
with me

Where I live I have met the wild spearmint and
plantain growing up negotiating cracks in cement;
The reason I stay is because I've met familiar people
without ever exchanging names, because I've found
beings who extend realities of family

How do you love a country?
You love the piece of Earth where you live
Love it fiercely, forgetting its forged
connections of
neighborhood, city, country
Love it fiercely,
Become relatives with the Birds
who will always sing with you if you
listen

which patent leather shoe belong to which found leg

1 COR 13:5 IF I GIVE AWAY ALL THAT I AM/ALL THAT I HAVE, AND IF I DELIVER MY BODY TO BE BURNED BUT HAVE NOT LOVE, I GAIN NOTHING

1 COR 13:7 LOVE BEARS ALL THINGS, BELIEVES ALL THINGS, HOPES ALL THINGS, ENDURES ALL THINGS

> *"Southern trees bear a strange fruit*
> *blood on the leaves and blood at the root*
> *...scent of magnolia sweet and fresh*
> *then the sudden smell of burning flesh..."*

30 years later and ahm sittin at a table
trying to make a poem out of 4 brown girls bombed outta they
skins
trying to make a poem about 4 brown girls sittin up in sunday school
singin Jesus Loves Me This I Know
learning "love is gentle, love is kind, love ain't puffed up"
what make me think i gotta right to make a poem about little girls
turning to smoke/turning to dust
on a sunday mornin/a great believin mornin
ahm talkin bout denise and cynthia
talkin bout addie mae
talkin bout carol
everybody know you ain't sposed to be talkin bout the dead, but they
wadn't but babies
trying to croon peace/trying to croon they way through
the waters
30 years later and ahm bout to start a funeral dirge cuz they was
sittin at the 16th street baptist church swingin too short legs
back and forth in pews and gigglin like kids do if they ain't
thinkin bout death   they wuz
thinkin bout what they wuz gonna do after sunday school/how
they wuz gonna sang in the choir/bout who they thought wuz cute
thinkin bout everything but being bombed outta they skins

singin
>wade in the water, wade in the water, children
>my gawd gon trouble deh water, my gawd gon trouble
>deh water

learning "love does not insist on its own way, love is gentle,
love is kind, love ain't puffed up"
they wuz wearing they sunday perfects to church/wearing they
all the time perfects to church/walkin
down the street to church in 4 pair of too tight patent leather
shoes
thinkin bout what to do after church and school on monday
wonderin bout baptism, gawd, and all
thinkin bout not puttin
a whole 50 cents in the collection plate
not thinkin bout being bombed outta they skins
not thinkin bout screamin
and they wuz singin some song bout
>i will thank the lord and praise his name forever, o lord
>i wouldn'tna made it this far, made it this far, made it
>if it had not been for the lord who is on my side
>the lord has

when it all came to a halt
when everything was charred and the pulpit was gone and the
choir loft
was gone
and the 4 girls addie mae collins
>carol robertson
>cynthia wesley
>denise mcnair

were charred and gone
cuz you know this is a funeral dirge and we got to say they names

this ain't no book/this ain't no newspaper talkin bout 4 girls
bombed in the
16th street baptist church/this ain't no headline fraid to say the
klan did it
the klan did it
we talkin bout cynthia and denise and addie mae and carol
we talkin bout 4 brown girls who wadn't goin
back to grade school on monday
we ain't talkin bout patent leather shoes just cuz somebody
wanna know
who shoe this is, which leg it belong to?
this here is a funeral dirge
30 years later
waiting for a song/a leaf/a somebody with an answer
waiting underneath all the new lynchings

> *"southern trees bear a strange fruit*
> *blood on the leaves and blood on the root"*

my girls are blk shadows lookin for an answer hangin
from a pulpit blown away
by the klan
september 15, 1963
birmingham, alabama
in a blk baptist church on 16th street
let us pour this libation
let us all say aché

sonnetblkbrwn #2

conversation

first light mockingbird sang   welcome
to america
home under siege where de   blue dey shoot
anything that mooves or grooves or shouts
where the indigenous fight for breathth

she said she was a
goddess
and she
was an everlasting queen home

come to dance in oyayu   from death;s
way of falsif;

fying de   meaning of life, the
me, the mean, demeaning of life

multiple assaults

Multiple generations of the same race on two continents are being infected. In sub-Saharan Africa and in Harlem, we have women, men, and children dying together in the same house.

multiple generations of the same race on two continents are being infected. in your crib and my crib on Amsterdam Avenue and on Times Square, on Christopher Street and on Fulton Street, we gots women, men, and children dying together in the same house.

the shit b funky

can you hear the base
can you hear the base
1 2 1 2 3 1 2 3 4 7 9 21
times   can you hear the base of his skull
hit the baton
hit the ground
can you hear the base of his skull
hit the ground you walk on sometimes

are you in tune with the groove
can you see the groove of her soul dancing
red through the glass shards he hit her with cuz
his skull hurt

can you get the rhythm of
over and over and over and over
again and again and again
of the groove and the base

"it's strictly base now," he said
"only freebase
  cuz needles in yo arms give you diseases that faggots got
  and they need them so they can die..."
  can you feel the base   can you get the groove now
  freebasin gon kill yo ass too
  and dead is dead is dead

and what if when you were down, i picked you up
i gave you my hand to grasp cuz i am strong
what if i fed you when you were hungry
and let you cry on my shoulder when your womon left
what if after all that we've been through,
what if i am a faggot
would you kill me then
would you say i manipulated you and touched you funny
would you get mad and kill me cuz i didn't tell you
you were crying on a faggot's shoulder cuz a
shoulder is a shoulder and a tear
is a tear
would you get mad and kill me cuz i didn't tell you
that you eating off a plate that i eat off too

and what if sistahs, what if i am a dyke
what will you do now
cuz before you might have said my hair
is nappy cuz i wanna b a man
but now that it's down to be black again and perms
don't define all that we are
now sistahs, what would you do to me if i am a dyke

would you not speak to me in the streets
would you hug your man extra tight when i walk by
what would you do on that late night
when i offer you a ride home
to your home and we start to talk
and we go to my home and talk all night
and when dawn comes up
you see audre's picture on my wall and jump up to leave
like ahm bout to pounce on you
and you say, "why didn't you tell me,
i wouldn'tna got in a car with you, bitch"
and you say, "why didn't you tell me,
i wouldn'tna come up in your crib, bitch"
and it didn't come up cuz all night we was talkin bout
lynching and burnings and povertys and revolt and what the fuck
didn't come up last night,
sistah

what would you do
if your little brother, your big sistah
yo uncle, yo mama, yo auntie, or your best friend from
way back when
came up to you
and said, "i'm dyin, i'm dyin, i got AIDS, won't you give me
some aide?"

would you say: faggot, get out my face
would you say: bulldagger, get out my way
would you say: sistah, brother, father, mama

move

brother, when you died/the name of the constellation

For Sabah as Sabah

I.

Indeed, death is in the blink of an eye
A particular moment when the last breath leaves
To circulate this earth elsewhere

When the eyes of the beholders reopen,
The lens' shift to negotiate newly barren spaces
The gaze tries to reconstruct the body from hazy shadows
and the remaining artifacts of photos and a few prominent
memories.
Those who arrive first or with grand technology or great
mourning decide to chart the picture of your life with a ruler.
With fingers wrapped around pencils, they map from Point A
to Point B and so on.
It is like drawing lines between stars to create The Great Bear
or Orion's Belt,
The images created do not often resemble the life or body that
encompassed the first and last breath.
If possible, it is best to leave behind all manuals, save what
the body said or wrote or drew—it is best to leave behind all
manuals when looking at the sky. What is left then are stars
and the space between them.

With the stars and the space between them, the life is a
masterpiece to behold because it shifts and changes year
round with what is remembered and what is forgotten, with
the familiar smell that wafts through a window bringing a
pleasant remembrance

II.
The first long months after you passed from harlem
to the next world
I could not remember anything except the wilting memories:
the wheelchair, the lesions, the yellow snot, the fact that we
didn't type up your poetry, the earth wind and fire box set you
had at your old aptment that I wanted, a trip we didn't take to
fire island, the day I forgot to bring the pink lemonade snapple
you were craving. I blocked out stars and charted only your
death which made your life unnavigable.

This morning I am filled with a great recollection:
You wrote love poems for straight Blk men and they said,
"Thank You." You led a life of curved notes and spirals and
deep bellied groans of pleasure and pain. You prayed with the
new morning, read the Holy Koran and you believed in Allah
and you loved life and you sashayed and you strutted and you
held men in your arms and you went down on men and men
danced with you in clubs and you cried if they left and if you
thought you might be able to love somebody you glowed and
you fucked men and you made love to men and when a fine
man walked in a room, you turned your head and you made
spells with childhood rhymes in your poetry which is still
delicious and now that I am remembering your living, your
death pales in comparison.
It is a million light years away from your laughter.

Still, I am watching as we all pick sharp shards or tiny slivers of
your truth to tell and sometimes in this we deny stars or spaces
in order to map the constellation of
our desire.

The drawing of our own constellations in rememberance of you
is not the problem. It is the times when some have rushed to plot
exact locations and marked
the spot of your life with permanent ink which only you should
have done.

Bearing Fruit

Today, I picked wild cherries.
This juice drips and beckons
and stains now now you take
over my rooms;

seep like lavender oil
everywhere   when you are gone
over a year now the wild
cherries are

bursting ripe, brother
weighting limbs down, falling
all over the sidewalk
brother, i stopped

and filled a mason jar

i miss you
echoes universes
and responds

1 year after yr death

did
you know your
father   has
thrown down the
scissors is
crying   your
umbilical cord
is hanging
onto the
mighty tail
of this comet which
    is
       memory
         and rising?

Rain Poem at 3am
for Arty Ann

"I miss hearing the rain
touch the ground," she said

Tonight when I hear it
my thoughts go to her
and I remember when I lived
on 124th and LaSalle and
the train rammed into my life
every 15 minutes and I
want to
tell her
now
even at this hour
how I miss Rain too
and
How growing up
we, 4 brown children on the avenue,
used to run outside in
the summer downpours
to be drenched in steamy wetness
and it was freedom then
toes wiggling in the mud
connected to feet
connected to ankles
steppin to the rhythm of ancient echoes,
            movin back
            movin back
hips, shoulders, arms, back, ass
grooving to previously unheard songs
uprising
from throats drinking elderspirit juice

we became blk children learning magic
speaking in tongues
spirit-sitting between present and past
the veil of skin between water and blood
disappearing between pages
of science

You see,
Rain was dropping her stories on the leaves of
Baobob trees, swimming through the ocean
she was sending her stories
up through mud and
we, like pigs, wallowed
in it

I, too, miss the Rain, sister
miss the sounds from my avenue

In this city, there are hardly any meeting
places for Dirt and Rain;
corporations have made
forts from umbrellas

We can walk
and not get wet
We think that this
is freedom

8 ways of looking at pussy

1.
enter here and find your home
your bathwater run already
the sun setting in the distance
heat on the horizon of your clit

2.
swollen pussy
all laid out and relaxed,
says to everyone in the room
"I have been to mecca and back
and it ain't nuthin compared to what you
done did"

3.
when you're wet and waiting
I could be lost six
universes away without a map
and sniff my way home

4.
baby, baby, hold still
my dreads are underneath
your thigh

5.
with those three brwn fingers inside,
you impregnate me with desire
I grow wide and wild
my water breaks,
this dam gives and we are tossing on the rapids
tossing on the rapids
overturning canoes,
water races out and over your arm

warm cum shoots out
races up your
arm, you put
your mouth
over this geyser

6.
I love like the ocean at first light
the waves coming in to meet the edges
of earth; rushing up and back like tiny orgasms
high tide the explosion
of you
on my
tongue

7.
my teeth on your nipple tastes sweet
I clench harder bite down on sensations
like acupuncture—I feel energy rising
connecting from
one hand/nearly elbow deep in your pussy
one hand over your mouth
your sister and my boy cousin
so close they can smell but
they snore instead. you giggle
I bite harder taste past skin
you giggle again.

8.
venus flytrap
eats me alive
everytime

poverty's monologue

I got this half-breed daughter named Poor. She was conceive during this one time the Sun got me to fuck her and she talked so nasty, she made me laugh. I mean, it just didn't seem natural at all. None of it. Not Sun coming round showing off her dark side luring me inside her eclipse that day. Because she always hated me as much as she can hate anything. I mean whenever my intimate calculations of how to drain somebody's life blood gets fucked up, it's always her that has something to do with that. She has snatched victims right out of my teeth when I was hungry. She has made me lose sleep.

So when she came talkin that, "Hey sweet Poverty, I know you wanna fuck me, I'm all wet for your hard rich dick thing." I thought, "Well, I'll be damned. Opposites do attract." There was a moment of hesitation. But She sent some of that what I thought was pussy smell into the wind and I pushed hesitation away from my groin. And for a moment I thought even if this is a game and this bitch thinks she can manipulate me I will teach her about the master and the slave. Not that I minded the game, I always did want to fuck the Sun, to hold her down and make her scream my name.

But it didn't turn out that way. She told me later—after the high huge tidal waves of laughter she made come running out of me and after I woke up sore but thinking I'd finally trained her ass, made her realize who the man is.

I mean I thought I had that bitch trained cuz she was screaming, "Pimp Daddy, Pimp Daddy, fuck me hard. Big man, fuck me like war, fuck me like crack cocaine, fuck me like welfare, fuck me like a schoolyard shooting, fuck me like a driveby. Give me all those drugs you deal, Poverty, Give em to me raw."

Anyway, turns out that Bitch made up the whole plan, even got that cunt Moon to be in on the deal. Told Moon to come cast a sultry shadow over her punani so I wouldn't know what I was sticking my dick in. Turns out Sun gave me just one of her rays and that no matter what my intent was—which like I said was to make her know I owned her—the fire and light of her was a refracting lens that made my powers inaudible to her pussy.

And when she woke me up to kick me out of her ray, I still felt like giggling even though I was pissed off and wanted to beat her black and blue, leave her trailing pus and blood throughout her journey in the sky. She had me giggling back to my office, even though I was planning all kinds of ways to kick her ass. Because I've been to college and she hasn't. I took anatomy and physiology and I know what a fucking pussy looks like and I've fingered many a crackhead and many a children and I've had my dick all up in multitudes of broke women who can't pay rent so we make a little exchange.

And Sun had me believing I was fucking her when she was making love to me. And for the first time I didn't get a souvenir from a bitch I fucked. Not a piece of hair, or spirit, or soul, not even the imprints of fear tracked down my back when a bitch scream cuz I'm fucking her life up so good. No, no souvenir because I didn't fuck her, as she pointed out, she fucked me and stole my shit. Had me giggling like those little children I steal laughter from when I give them tears and hardness in their chests, she said all that those "pimp daddys" I heard was my imagination.

Sun had the guts to tell me that the only words she said during the whole eclipse of our time together were: "Life, Living, Live." And she said that I was repeating that shit, repeating it loudly. And I don't want to think about that because that would mean I was being hoed.

And she said it was the first time she ever saw me smile without that blood dripping from my mouth and that when I came I let all these people go. I said, "Oh, shit, does that mean Mumia and Peltier are free?" She said, "Yes, Hallelujah," while she did a little dance that made me hard again and I had to stifle because if I didn't she could pilfer my entire kingdom away. And Sun was still talking while I was trying to make my dick go down and thinking of ways to murder her.

"And in your eyes, Poverty, in your eyes, and it almost made me love you for a minute, I saw you grow gardens in the Marcy Projects, I saw you wipe this old woman's tears away and take that bottle of 5-O from Eldridge Johnson. But I knew it was a fuck thing and I had this little espionage job to do on you Poverty, so get on out my Ray go think about how good I make you feel with one little itsy bitsy powerful piece of me. You ain't shit, Poverty. And by the way, little dick, I'm gon have a baby and she gon kick yo ass on the daily."

So that was about 9 years ago and I am constantly looking behind my self. Checking my pockets, my credit cards, my bank account, and my conscience to make sure I'm not getting soft. I mean, I do get the urge to go back and get some of that laughter but I can't have everything and I get high off watching people come screaming my name and Sun she wouldn't do that. So I stay doing what I do because I can take vacations to hot places like my partner Pain's crib and make believe it's her heat. Sometimes, I just go and take away everything a person's got: the job, the family, the hoopty, the orange juice in the refrigerator, all dreams, sometimes I make bald patches appear on people's heads, or I snatch all the teeth and songs from their mouth. Sometimes I bite down so hard on somebody's dreams that they spit them out into my hand and I crush them in front of their face. I do this to keep hard, to keep from laughing, cuz I like to hear them scream my name to beg for that trick Mercy.

Now, Poor, I must say she's a gorgeous child and I wish I had been powerful enough that night so she could be for real dangerous like me. But she makes the people I fuck with smile. I mean, this little girl is always coming up, sneaking round the corner when I leave people on their scraped knees spitting up blood and she's showing them double rainbows and taking them on long walks till they find their song again. It's a constant battle between me and her and she's only nine.

I do try to think of ways to make her my daughter. Like once when she was two, I had her thinking free cheese and butter and welfare stamps and free and reduced lunch were all great things for people. But her mother put a end to that with quickness I heard her bellowing loud and clear: "Poor, stop handing that bullshit to those people, that butter ain't real, it cain't ease no pain." All the while I'm trying to yell over Sun, "Poor, that's it baby girl, hand it to em, they like those clogged veins makes em feel full." But Sun showed her a seed of something and next thing I know, Poor got all these folks I took houses from, all these ignorant, dumb niggers and rednecks, and spicks and shit whose stuff I threw out on the street. She has them following her to these empty lots and planting seeds in the ground and when I see that I get so tired and know that Poor is her mama's child with her mama's energy and I drudge on home to jack my self off and remember laughter.

54

Memory
  For Renita

your fingerprints
are on my memory
from way back
when
        you were and still are the wind
and I was dust on your fingertips
you blew
me round
into a frenzy then
          like now
when your brilliance makes my cells holyghost

our love is more ancient than the milky way
it is a holy temple
a circular clearing in trees

though how we love is mighty
I am not deceived by its danger
since we have been here before
have died doing our work before now
I remember you were christ's left palm,
harriet's stamina, hawk's wings

I remember the work we do is still everlasting;
keep your fingerprints in my memory as reminder

Rhonda, Age 15 Emergency Room

...Yeah, I been to juvee, what about it?
I was up at Spofford—they got legends
bout me—thought they wasn't gon git
rid a me, but yo I had to git de fuck up
outta dere, they had hoes that murder
people in that piece
and
I'm baaad and all but I ain't never
murdered nobody yet and I try not
to fuck up nobody too much less
they mama cain't recognize em

Last night, my man Ray-Ray, he 23
and built better than buster douglass
well anyway, we was over to his
crib and he was tryin to git on
for some
but he been locked up for 4 months
and I 'ont know what that nigga
been doin—shit, I know what
I was doin up in Spofford—
so when I tole him I was having my
menstruals, he decided to get plexed.
He smoked a blunt and wouldn't
take me home and den the nigga
went n fell asleep.
I was like damn, here I am
at Ray-Ray's crib and I got
a motherfuckin curfew and a
math test tomorrow (I'm tryin
to do good in school for probation
and dis lady who teach English

say I got potential—which I did
look up in the dictionary. It mean
I gots mad promise if my ass don't
end up in jail).

So I'm lookin for a pencil,
anything to write on which,
when I find it, is a paper towel
and thinkin that Ray-Ray ain't
helpin me none and he must
be a stupid nigga to boot cuz
he ain't got no paper and I
had to sharpen the pencil
wit a knife. I starts to think
bout findin me a new man.

Me and my math problems
plexin each other to death,
when Big Mac come knockin.
He Ray-Ray's cousin
so I let him in. He say,
                    where Ray-Ray?
I'm like he sleepin, he blunted out—
            Ah, he say, *you wanna watch a movie*

I look at the napkin, crunch it
up, make a perfect 3 pointer and
follow Big Mac to the living room.
He put in the tape and turn off the
light. Then the movie come on
and at first I'm fixin to git up cuz
this ain't my kind of movie—girls
in all kinds of crazy positions suckin

white boys off, bitches lettin em
whip they ass and tie em up. That's
at first, cuz the next thing I know
I'm feelin crazy shit go through me:
       cunt juice drippin down
       my leg and I'm freakin
       myself out cuz i thought
       that shit only happen at
       Spofford. Cuz I'm imaginin
       I'm stompin all the white
       boys. Walkin up to em
       while dey whippin dem
       girls and I'm stickin .45s in
       dey back—but that ain't all.
       I'm thinkin after I kill em,
       de ladies gon want to fuck
       me, and yeah, that's the part
       I'm trippin on, that I want
       them to fuck me and that
       Ray-Ray didn't never make me
       feel like the cuties in juvee.

And I look over at Big Mac to see
if he know yet by the look on my face that
I'm a fuckin homo. Cuz if he don't know yet
I want to fix my face before he guess.
And when I look at him I'm like
I know this nigga done lost his mind cuz
the bitch is sittin there with his dick
outta his pants and his hand movin all
fast n shit and he stop when he see me,
den he start talkin real deep bullshit

he say,

> Rhonda come here, Why don't you
> do me, Come on Rhonda do me.
> Ray-Ray ain't gonna mind, I ain't
> gonna tell him.

He reach over and
touch my titty and me, ms. bad ass
all of a sudden cain't move
I'm frozen, I mean I couldn't move
> damn you cute
> girl, I wanna git my groove
> on wit you, I always...

The nigga
stop talkin then.
He all grunts and shit and I'm
imaginin I'm on another planet
tryin to think about the math test
and that lady-teacher I got
and I feel all that POTENTIAL
running the fuck away
cuz I won't claw this nigga to death
cuz I cain't even believe it's happenin
cuz he Ray-Ray's cousin and
cuz i ain't never felt no pain like this
so I don't feel it/I/think/bout/this/
time/I/beat/this/bitch/so/bad/she/lost/
6/teeth/and/got/scars/to/this/day/
from/the/box/cutter/I/slashed/cross/
her/face/

I guess he done cuz he start to say
somethin
> don't worry girl, I know you...

And I don't hear the mothafucka
finish cuz I'm outta the room and
shakin Ray-Ray so hard he think
it's a earthquake in Bed-Stuy.
I make
that nigga
git up
and take
me home
in his mama's
raggedy-ass hoopty.

And I start cryin
when I see my projects
and commence to tellin
Ray-Ray everything.
First thing he do is say,
>   *hell naw, you my bitch,*
>   *ahm a take care of this shit.*
Den he tell me to take a bath
and he gon call me after he settle
this shit.
Then he leave.
I let myself in and hope mama ain't wake.
She ain't.
I go to de bathroom,
flick de light on,
watch de roaches git
de fuck out my way,
and set the water to run.
I wuz gonna take a real
hot bath, but I
membered too

late we ain't got
no hot water right now.
So, I pullt the drain
and went to bed.
But all I'm thinkin
bout is my test
and my potential—
how ahm gon git it back—
so I find the damn book
and jist study and study and study
till round bout 7:30 when
I'm still wide awake and
fixin to go to the school.

For the first time I'm gon
make first period.
I'm steppin out the door and I see
Ray-Ray walkin up,
he look real mad.
I don't feel nothin but
good cuz I know I can
pass. He git closer and I
smell malt on him. He say,
  I see you like them clothes, bitch
and I member right
then that I ain't changed
he say it again,
  yeah, you like the fuck smell on dem clothes.
I go
  you crazy nigga, I ain't like shit about yo cousin

he like,

> you lyin cunt, Big tole me de
> whole story, He say you wanted to fuck him,
> He say you come over to him while he
> tryin to watch a movie and put
> your hand on his dick and
> He say he told you he wasn't gon
> disrespect me like that but you kept
> touchin on him and I cain't blame the nigga
> for goin for his. I cain't believe you did that
> shit, Rhonda. You spose to be my girl and you
> go fuckin my cousin.

He got me backed up in
the corner in the lobby. People
see us and don't nobody say shit.
I don't say shit again cuz ahm in
shock and de only thing I'm thinkin
is bout how
to figure $x=y^2$
when he say,

> you ain't got nothin to say, bitch?

> the way to solve $x=y^2$ was
> still runnin through my mind
> when he hit me and I fell down
> and I felt him kickin math answers
> out my head.
> I got sad cuz I wadn't gon' make
> first period and my POTENTIAL
> act like it ain't never comin back.

when

burned bodies
beneath blue break
blood, cloud my wings
to stone

and anger
comes clawing in
connects, cements
my song

to four walls
with no windows
baby, you sun
me back

through midnight's
shadow, feather
slow my ashes
into

dancing stars
you say, even
roaring oceans
of my

spirit name
quiet among
my tears; you wing
imagination

into five
eagles dancing
drunk on sky's
ceiling

I listen
to stubborn flapping

Claw myself into
flight

Freedom is

Freedom is a hard bop to follow cuz the way it weaves
Cuz that way it weaves ain't
Ain't nuthin like slave shackles on your ankles
        slave shackles on your ankles keeping

                                you sinking

down

            into whatever
                        keeps you
                        down
I mean how can you follow
        skeaweebop
                didskeaweetipbop
                        befreedobefree
                                gobefreebopsizz bop
                                sizz
                                sizzdadasizzdofreemamafree
unless you be concentrating
                        on the sound

how it sliiiiiiiide

                                        through
keyholes....

Talking bout
talking bout how
how we is here
        n   still 'live
                though hanging on
                        gobefree

                                gobefree

64

bopbaloobalootriplet!

       sizz.
       n still 'live
           though hanging on
           to some remembered strand
                    of some motherland songs.

Freedom be
       sneaking
       into prison on callused hands and feet
       Sawing
           bars off windows.
       Whispering urgently
           to all prisoners

diphop

triplet
       a kera washington groove flows off in all directions
                    triple

triplet

                   whispering

     Climb Through

skeaweetata
     Climb through

            boodadadafree
         climb through

car alarms

car alarms go off before we do
and time, da revolution be done almost passed us by
but we b too busy wearin kente cloth, makin up handshakes,
buyin red/blk/green toaster oven covers and shit like that
and time, da revolution b done
passed us by almost
but we b in style
and we b playin b-ball, smokin blunts
and stealin or buyin
cars and
alarms, car alarms go off before we do
and we b in style
but we still b dyin

car alarms go off before we do
and it only b a thunderstorm
that sets them off—a whole neighborhood
of them, our cars
protesting cause something natural, like a rainstorm
got a little too close
but we need to b a little like car alarms
and go off at all the unnatural shit invading us
we need to go off, people
we need to be an off people
an off the beaten track people
and get out of cars and walk people
a touch ground people
a touch dirt people
we need to go off, people
at all the stuff surrounding us
cuz a month ago yetta adams died, people
on a bench outside
in the cold, people

and we didn't go off
we went inside and got warm.
might have turned on the tv or the radio and said, "damn the
system"
but we didn't go off, people
like terry taylor when he turned the mirror back on those cops in
tompkins
square
we need to be an off people/a go off people/a fight back people
we just need to see, people
that no one can do it for us, but us
in all our complexions, in all our complexities, in everything we
have
with our bare hands and raw voices, and we can do this
we can go off
now
cuz it's cold outside
and we still dyin
and the war still rages

Cocaine grab-ded me
for T.B.

jumping out of a
burning building is hard
to get used to
especially if that building sticks to you
like poverty—keeps you run
ning
and
run
down

to jump or not to jump out of a burning building
is a hard choice
when all you know
is flames licking
inside your soul and the smell of singed skin
no matter how many times you beat flames
into submission

jumping from anything as high as you've been, girl
could be dangerous
since you can't always remember what jagged edges you threw
from
windows
since you can't know if anyone who's still around will catch you
or your
tears
when you get your feelings back
or if jumping means breaking yo ass/dying a whole
nuther way
since you can't know if jumping means
that the building might crumble down
on your back

leaving final wails
and dust
in your absence
and nothing

and nothing
and nobody
to speak
the whys and how comes
it has to come to
this
i mean nobody
to say
that your mother beat you
and your father beat you
and your sister didn't speak to you
nobody and nothin
left
to say that it all came to this
cuz you was following orders to
be all you could be
and quickly discovered
that it
meant
you were a
young
blk dyke
alone on the streets
at 14
and some addicts
are nice people
wanna be your friend
don't give a fuck who you fuck
long as you got some money

jumping from a burning building that is your skin is necessary

BURN
your ashes will compost
and you will
rise
rise up
singing morning songs
of healing

jumping out
jumping out
of your own skin
into your own
song is sometimes
necessary
to get
yo
skin
back,
sister

girl,
please jump
now
fo' I miss
you
again

Untitled Bliss

when she comes, i am
tornado's eyes,
a hurricane takes my
brain and swirls it into
unspeakable colors of sky and
land and volcano rushes up to
meet the sound of her and lava
runs down my marrow pulling
me further into oblivion. It is
this hot. We molten new
forms; new entities.
We travel seven planets
beyond this one when she comes and
my fist or my tongue
or my spirit is inside
her, we are one
sunrise; red and orange in
soft air, we are one hawk
circling wide winged over the
canyon—one song, i hear
over in my head, "you dropped a
bomb on me" by the Gap band and
it is like this too: I die and
am reborn/ashes again/
reborn.   i see
through the walls.

blksestina

for nirmalani ngozi abiaka

Adenenye's sleep was filled with heavy rain and dirt
slipping through cracks in the ceiling from mountain
while an elder sat in the rainforest twisting magic
in her locks, and songs which would not be called music
here rose from her inclining ants and goddesses to dance
like blues in the flame of fire

With hot colors swirling down the mountain she met fire
She walked outside barefooted, her toes mingling with cool dirt
Adenenye felt the plum colored elder call her to dance
She saw the sunrise and followed her up the mountain
There, she saw a goddess playing djembe to the elder's music
Adenenye dove headfirst into the waves of magic

Coming through the song, she became magic
Laughter flowing through her entire body, she was on fire
inside and everything—the water, her footsteps, the stones—had
                    its own music
The rhythms all ancient as dirt
She stood watching a goddess sift dreams through her earth
                    brown hands over an edge of mountain
Dreams dusting over like snowflakes made her want to dance

Adenenye became the wind when she started to dance
She also conjured ghosts and spirits with her swaying side-to-side
                    magic
It was an old-fashioned revival up there on the mountain
Cuz Adenenye had waded through fire and found dirt
underneath her pores that tasted like music

She found she could make music
Just by exhaling—making her nasal hairs dance
Just by drawing a circle with her toe in the dirt
The goddesses knew Adenenye's magic
They had long ago walked through the dreaming fire
Into the mountain

Heavy dreams and dirt fell from the mountain
while an elder with skin like red clay plucked music
into her locks with songs that burned blue like fire
and Adenenye opened her eyes in slumber to dance
and pour from her own hands magic
black and deep as dirt

Adenenye awoke to dirt underneath her tongue and stones in her
bed from a mountain
of magic piled up inside her and the music
dripping from her eyes was the ocean she had danced through to
meet fire

2:45 Possession

the furies
came hard
came fast
rushing
to meet
birthsong
rising
up from
red dreams
like lava
gushing through a
rhythm-
and-blues
mind; an
old man
sitting
on the
front stoop
drinking
and
snapping
his fingers
snap
to music
snap

there's a
green gypsy
who stops
round here
daily,
stands in
the middle

of blue hill
road
twirls around
dancing
sending
gusts of
wind in
his direction
        snap
he thinks
        snap
he knows
        snap
he is seeing
a not real
thing—a mirage
or a ghost
        snap
but he
        snap
always
drops his
bottle
breaks on the concrete
but he
keeps
snapping
his fingers
in time w/the
jump slide twirl
spring slide
twirl summer
seasons change when

she does
    snap
she dances
    snap
she brings up
supreme furies
    snap
incites riots
in his cells
    snap
she dances
    snap
his name everyday
until she stops
everyday
and he stops
snapping
shuffles
down to
People's
Liquor
Store.

Harlem Haiku

white chalk outlines girl's
extensions left on pavement
mother's souvenir

spring rain drops slowly
natty boy sits down on curb
grinning into clouds

young boys on corner
throw caution and three dice hard
against project wall

roaches day sojourn
from sink back to cabinets
begins at first light

he who's she and tall
tap taps blood red fingernails
waiting for coffee

whites nearly fall out
leaning from tour bus windows
shooting their pictures

music and spliff smoke
indulge us as we dance on
way past the midnight

Beginning Therapy

I won't touch
just tiptoe along edges of the nucleus of pain
shy away at the slightest sting
retreat
then creep up to dive into the mitochondria
where the source of my breath
and my mother's breathing lies
I need to know this   this deep
darkness where my birth and death
play poker with each other.
I need to
watch this game, lean over
death's shoulder; peeking at the cards

Afterbirth

Tell me if they told you
your mother was dead and pulled you
away screaming from a makeshift grave

then assembly lined and marched you assembly
lined to cut down your sister trees put earth's blood
in water, replaced your horizon with billboards

Tell me if they (or you)
covered your body with pretense
for eachevery ceremony
following birth
how would you

know

to find home?

      Let me tell you—

      Upstairs knitting holy the
      song torn from our bodies,
      there is a guiding star of ages,
      who answers questions in
      your dreams

           you've seen her
           during thunderstorms
           bent over
           that flaming web of truth
           between screaming
           and seductive numbness

you've seen her
open her mouth to receive
fire

Listen cousin,

if you ask, she will mirror
your skin is enuf clothing
is enuf to keep you
to keep you warm
most of the time

she knows how to reach
that place past cold discordance

      if you know you are
      lost, she can tell you
      your heart beats the rhythm
      of your house
      gives you cadence to knit
      your self the long road home
      she will tell you
           your
           heart
           is
           muscle you
           been exercising
           the wrong way for
           years
           you gotta flex
    where your heart homes you

if you call and listen with each
and every dream each and every
muscle, she will leave notes
on the back of your eyelids
on the moss of treebark
in the blueblack feather of crow
          telling you

          we are all born knowing
          how to reach toward sun
          to crave earth
                    to dance
                    air into
                    lungs
                    to seek water after
                    our mothers' breasts

          all our relations

          do you remember when they
          dragged you away
          screaming
          do you remember
          yo mama's song to you
          do you 'member
          she sang everything
          everything
          I have is yours

For Emilie

"You have to commit to a garden."
—Donna Weber

some folks are like fertile soil
the kind of dark moist dirt you hold
between your fingers knowing that
the difference between skin and dirt
is fierce imagination

I imagine you the right amount
of rainforest, desert, quicksand, and
religion

Operation Urgent Fury

Lately these nights find me awake and listening for air raids;
the low hum of airplanes over this house and the pictures
of Palestinian children in line for gas masks and soldiers in Tel Aviv
leave me restless.   But in the daylight, I am still making lists of
things to do and taking my time to cook dinner.   This difference is
an unreconcilable gulf.

This place where america has us is right where he wants us
When is the last time you touched dirt?
How is it that the president's penis commands more attention than
the sun rising, his hard-on can take us away from business at hand?
(no pun intended—except he can kill two birds with one stone just
by jacking off on your tv screen)

Headline Line Up For Head
41 millions dollars spent 41 million american dollars spent and
it doesn't even add up to me or anyone else searching for just one more
dollar to pay the rent or just 42 more cents to get a cup of coffee or
a thumb
nail size bottle of tequila but
whose head is at the front of the line to get paid
and whose heads are at the front of the line to die

and remember when america jacks off, he leaves you hanging with the
responsibilities
america is a deadbeat dad
america is a rapist
fucks us without asking, incites terror, holds open the walls of our
cunts
running trains on us, running trains on us

All Aboard

All Aboard
        next stop Panama
        next stop Mexico
        next stop East St. Louis
        next stop Persian Gulf
All Aboard to Detroit

If you got a ticket you can get on this train
If you got a penis and your credit has no limit, you can get a ticket

All Aboard, Gentlemen
Did you bring your checkbooks to clean up the mess after
these ejaculation contests   Did you bring the bony fingers of
hunger starved hands and give them dustpans   Did you bring
the megaphones and the platforms to stand and holler: SWEEP

Did you bring the muzzles

All Aboard to Grenada
All Aboard Para la immigracion
All Aboard to WorkFare
        next stop Vietnam
        next stop Korea
        next stop Tuskeegee
        next stop South Africa
        next stop Birmingham
        next stop Nicaragua
        next stop
Get on Board Gentlemen Get on Board
        next stop Iraq

Headline Line Up For Head
Saddam is a crazy man
he's so crazy we can't even pronounce his name

it's hunting season, nobody runs a thousand trains with us
and then quits
                next stop Indianapolis
Smart Bomb em with multicolored crack vials
All Aboard to Cuba
All Aboard for Nigeria
All Aboard Rwanda

america is a wife beater a homohater a stalker
an antienvironmentalist america is a dangerous machine
america makes you/makes me
makes us part of the machinery: are you a ball bearing
or a piece of virtual
memory
am I an axle or a factory belt

I woke up this morning and I brushed my teeth with Crest
made Dunkin Donuts coffee and I put on a shirt and did not think
about where it was made and I did not look at the sky this morning
and when I turned the heat up last night I did not think about who
was dying
in the cold
I was not thankful   I complained about the oil bill
and I did not think this morning about joy and I did not think this
morning
about anything but
my first cup of coffee
I did not think this
morning about bombs reigning down on dreams and dreamers
I logged onto aol and did not
think about bombs until I looked up Vietnam
and Mohammed Ali and found most of the pages
are mysteriously unavailable

understand america

we want life
to rampantly course
through cemented fields of rhetoric

to blood this home
of violent dry wounds
where soulified ghosts (still)

stand on breath's peninsula
beckoning voice

heart   trees   stone   rain   flaming

the people's bones are thirsting for sunrise.

these dreams anxious volcanoes
puncture sleep, change earth
forever

comrades, here
is the edge of the dying sun

        where

        we
        must

        riot

        into memory;

        rain
        bow

        every
        thing

juba

for renita

u be a gospel song
some a dat
ole time religion
where the tambourine git goin
and the holy ghost sneak up
inside people's bones and
everybody dancin and shoutin
screamin and cryin
oh jesus, oh jesus
and the people start to clappin
and reachin back to african rhythms
pulled through the wombs of
the middle passage
and women's hats start flying
while the dance,
the dance they do gets hotter and holier
and just the music has brought cause for celebration

yeah, u be a gospel song, girl
like some a dat ole back in the woods, mississippi river kinda
gospel
and i feel the holy ghost when you is
inside me
and the tambourines keep goin
and folks is stampin they feet
and oh no,
it's the neighbor knocking on the door
askin is we alright
say we was screamin
oh jesus, oh jesus
and i heard us but i
didn't hear cuz

i was being washed in the gorgeous wetness of
your pussy
being baptized w/ole time religion
the oldest religion there
is
2 women inside the groove
of each other
we come here
we come
we come here
to be
saved

ACKNOWLEDGMENTS

When I was growing up, relatives, friends of parents, and sometimes strangers would ask the obligatory "What do you want to be when you grow up?" I always said, "A teacher and a writer." I want to acknowledge the people and beings who believed me and helped me to believe in my self. Please know that the writing of *Juba* would not have been possible without your help and your "intimate witnessing" of this journey.

Thanks to:
Johanna Amefia-Koffi, Seana Murphy, Jenny Robertson, Breshaun Joyner, Ruth Tiederman, Sara Gaskell, Mike Church, Angela Walters, Noname aka Nick Cabot, Sara Levin, Ali Liebegott, Steve Fried, Chris Lew, Regie Cabico, Marilyn Kaggan, Cheryl Boyce Taylor, Kim Horne, Guillermo Felice, Tony Medina, Amy Kuroiwa, Lourdes Follins, Carol Guess, Rich Perry, Barbara Lawrence, Rachel Levitsky, Amatul Hannan, Jue Hyen, Susan Woodfill, Michael Lassel, Nadine Mozon, Shawn Alexander, Bill & Nancy Teiderman, Melinda Goodman, C.D. Collins, Jaclyn Friedman, Tina D'Elia, Amina Baraka, Mike Ladd, Sonia Sanchez, Hannah Doress, Emily Bender, Tia Juana Malone, Lula Christopher, Crasta Yo, Kera Washington, Ifé Franklin, Clariessa Clay, Elise Harris, Vanessa Olivacce, Lisa King, Shoshana Rosenfeld, Eva Boyce, Abe Rybeck, Lisa King, Lauren & Dan Thomas-Paquin, Thomas Grimes, T'Kalla, Yvette Davila, Broderick Hunter, Layding Kaliba, Eliot Sloan, Judy Pennywell, Staci Rodriquez, Nelson Alexander, Lindsay Brown, Antonieta Jimenez, Jenna Spears, Nancy Lunsford, Donna Weber, Sierra Kahn, Christina Duvalier, Cassandra Cato-Louis, Rossette Capportorto, Jenny Hubbard, Emily Chang, Craig Bailey, Taj Bobbit, Robin White, Imani Henry, Lisa Owens, Jim Brough, Lynne Mendes, Stephanie Landry, Luke Caswell, Betsey Andrews, Katherine Durst, Sheila Stowell, Maria Aguiar, Girlfriends, Mocaa, Black Star Express, Shades of Lavender, The Audre Lorde Project, PAVE youth at Magnolia Tree Earth Center, students at the Agassiz School in Jamaica Plain, MA & in Marilyn Kaggen's class in Redhook, Brooklyn, The Gathering, Bromfield Street Educational Foundation, The New York Foundation for Arts, the Barbara Deming Money for Women Fund; Maya, Ramón, Melinda & Ronald Neely—and C.J. Chenier.

Thanks to everyone whose name I left on the editing room floor. It's the typesetter's fault.

Thanks to the folks who directly aided in *Juba* with copy editing, food, feedback, scanning, money, etcetera: Pia Infante, Teresa Lau, Imani Uzuri, Asha Bandele, Nadine Jones, Hanna Bordas, Miko Rose, Carla Richmond, Blue Heron, Nirmalani Ngozi Abiaka, and Kathy Brough.

Thanks to laurie prendergast for the long nights and days of book design.

Thanks to Emilie Delphinos Brough for insisting that I take the time and care to do my "work."

Thanks to Renita Martin for her love of words, fried okra, and our love.